Remembering Barbara Niblett
who made Burford Playgroup
a happy place – J.W.

Text copyright © 2001 by Jeanne Willis. Illustrations copyright © 2001 by Mark Birchall

The rights of Jeanne Willis and Mark Birchall to be identified as the author and illustrator of this
work have been asserted by them in accordance with the Copyright, Designs and Patents Act, 1988.
First published in Great Britain in 2001 by Andersen Press Ltd., 20 Vauxhall Bridge Road,
London SW1V 2SA. Published in Australia by Random House Australia Pty.,
20 Alfred Street, Milsons Point, Sydney, NSW 2061. All rights reserved.
Colour separated in Italy by Fotoriproduzione Grafiche, Verona.
Printed and bound in Singapore by Tien Wah Press.

10   9   8   7   6   5   4   3   2   1

British Library Cataloguing in Publication Data available.

ISBN 0 86264 901 3

This book has been printed on acid-free paper

Python
goes to Playschool

Written by Jeanne Willis
Pictures by Mark Birchall

Andersen Press • London

It was Python's first day at playschool.
"Be good," said her mother. And off she went.
"What shall I do now?" thought Python.

"Find someone to play with,"
said the teacher.

So Python went into the Wendyhouse.

SQUEAK! SQUEAK! SQUEAK! SQUEAK!

"Miss! Mi...iss! Python is squeezing Rat," shouted Weasel.

The teacher spoke very firmly to Python.
"You are not to squeeze," she said.
"Rat doesn't like it."
"What do I do now?" thought Python.

"Storytime," said the teacher.
Everybody sat on the floor and
listened quietly. Then, just as the story
was getting to the exciting bit . . .

SQUEAL! SQUEAL! SQUEAL! SQUEAL!

"Miss! Mi...iss! She's doing it again,"
shouted Weasel.

The teacher stopped reading and spoke very strictly to Python.

"You must not squeeze," she said. "It is unpleasant. Rabbit does not like it."

"What now?" thought Python.

"Plasticine!" said the teacher. "We're going to make plasticine snakes."

Python went over to the plasticine table.

For a moment all was quiet.

Then there was the most terrible bellowing and harrumphing and hissing you have ever heard.

"Miss! Mi...iss!" shouted Weasel.

"What is it now? Is Python squeezing somebody?" said the teacher.

"No, Miss. Somebody is squeezing Python!"
It was Elephant.

"Python was lying on the table and I mistook her for a piece of plasticine," Elephant explained.

After that, Python behaved beautifully.

Her mother arrived to take her home.
    "How did she get on with the others?"
she asked.
    "Oh . . . very squeezily," said the teacher.